Collection of Short Horror Stories

Written by C. M. Thomas

TO DIANE!

C. M. Thomas

Behind Closed Doors

"YOU'RE NEXT. YOU'RE NEXT." The horrible sound kept ringing in Sarah's ears. It was a splattered bug on her windshield, that she had gotten rid of properly but Sarah Jane Scott's story was not forgotten by a soul. It was not forgotten to never stay home alone. Back when Sarah went to college she didn't have a boyfriend. Not ever. Her parents died in a tragic accident. But that is another story. Sarah had to learn how to live by herself. And she did. For many years. But one night was unforgettable. It was snowing hard outside. School was canceled.

The power was out. All she had was a heavy-duty, orange-yellow black light. At this point, Sarah was considering suicide. She was so lonely. It was only later, an hour later, when she heard the noise. Coming from the living room. She knew the routine. She knew what was happening. Burglary. Sarah quickly but quietly grabbed a knife from the kitchen and snatched her black light. She made her way to the living room. As she turned the corner she wailed of fright. But there was nothing there. She was expecting more than an empty living room. She then heard another noise. From the window. It sounded like a hook scraping. She opened the curtains and then she had a reason to scream. A rotten, ugly dead body was hanging from a hook right on her window. She knew the first thing to do: call 911 on her rotary phone. But the power was out. She knew not to touch it. As she was about to walk away, Sarah noticed a note pinned on the body. It said in big bold letters, "YOU'RE NEXT." It was too scary. She had to turn the other way. Sarah slowly turned back around--but the body was gone. Gone. Gone. She heard the same hook scraping noise from her Christmas wreath on the outside of her front door. She ran over and shrieked. In the hole of the Christmas wreath, the same body's head was poking through. She ran and turned the corner to her bedroom and cried out. The body was hanging right there. Sarah ran and hid under the dining room table. She still had the knife and black light. Her black light started to flicker. The fifteenth time it turned back on, she screamed, for the body was hanging through the two X-shaped table legs. It seemed to be reaching for her. She scrambled out from under that table possibly faster than any human. Sarah heard a little sliding noise, much similar to that of an insect crawling. It was coming from the slight space between the light bulb and the light bulb socket. It was a note. A folded up piece of paper. Wedged in between. She reached up to grab it. She quickly pulled it down. She slowly unfolded it. Then--she saw it said "FIND OUT THE SECRET OR YOU'RE NEXT." What was absolutely terrifying about it was the message, but also the ink. The ink was blood. She looked back at the body. Still there.

But then Sarah noticed that there was a cut on the body, one which had not been there before. That meant--in a matter of seconds someone had cut the body--which seemed like a jackknife cut--there was someone else here. Sarah quickly looked around then looked at the dining room table--gone. Again. A sudden noise from behind her startled her out of her confused daze and she slowly turned around. But there was no body. The body was gone, that was an inevitable fact. Sarah was so confused and scared, she let out a quick sob. But then she noticed a note where the body used to be. It read, "1:23:46." Sarah thought it was some kind of code. Then, she realized, it was time. She knew she had one hour, twenty-three minutes and forty-six seconds before she's "next." She strongly wanted to know "the secret." After all, she was decidedly next. Next. Next. She thought she saw a woman dash across the room. Then she heard a prolonged, echoed, ghastly voice say, "Sarah, there's no reason to be afraid. It's me." This voice talked in a slow, depressive way, as if it was stuck in the depths of the underworld. Sarah sobbed, "My mother! I want my mother!" "Yes," the voice said calmly. She felt a jackknife slide into her ribcage. She screamed in agony. "The secret. Find. The secret." the voice said. *I forgot about the secret*, thought Sarah. "Can you give me a clue?" Sarah asked the voice. "Yes," the voice said,

"The secret is who I am. Find it out in one hour, twenty minutes, and ten seconds. Goodbye." And the voice ceased. She pondered. "I know who you are. You're the devil, aren't you?" She waited quite a while for a reply, but unfortunately no noise was heard. Sarah swore. "No, please!" the voice cried out. "You have to!" a dark, satanic voice called out. "What do you think? Then it would all be my fault. I won't. I refuse. Wait--what are you doing? Stop! No!" What followed was a loud scream and a thump, as well as a dragging sound. She knew that the woman voice was dead. Then, she had a flashback. of her mother. Her voice. The satanic voice killed her mother. The first time and the second. "Who are you? You lying

freak! WHO ARE YOU?" Sarah
yelled. "I am--" the demonic voice
started. "Well?" Sarah exclaimed,
out of breath. "You should know
who I am." droned the satanic
voice. Sarah pondered again.
Satanic, she thought, *the voice was
satanic.* "Satan. Just like I said
earlier." Sarah said. "You got it!"
Satan chuckled, "If you've ever
wondered how your mother died, I
hanged her!" Suddenly, all the
lights turned on. A red figure, with
a trident and claws and baring
teeth. Satan. With a pointed tail.
Satan. Then Sarah noticed a rope
wrapped around her mother's neck,
who was about 5 feet above the
ground. Sarah then remembered
her knife. She swung it out of her

pocket. "This is for my mother." Then she threw her arm at Satan and sliced his head. Satan laughed. "You'll die very soon! Remember when your mother cut you with the jackknife? I made her!" Sarah looked down at her cut. It was oozing blood. She was still in shock. "Goodbye, Sarah--" She ran to the bathroom. She got out all the towels she had, locked the door, and pulled out the hydrogen peroxide. She unscrewed the lid and poured some on a towel. She then dabbed at the wound lightly. She used another towel to get rid of some of the blood. Then Sarah grabbed some medical gauze and wrapped it around her rib area, tying it tight. She realized that if the jackknife was rusty, she could get tetanus.

She unlocked the door and went out. "I'm not afraid. I know the secret." The rest of the house when she came out was red. The walls had been mysteriously painted red. There was strange red fog low on the ground. Satan was taking over. "I know the secret too," Satan explained, "and I know that you know the secret. I told you that you had a certain amount of time before you're next. And that your death would be delayed if you found out. I have made a decision and you are still going to be next."
"What? I thought we had a deal!" Sarah exclaimed. "You never agreed to it." Satan had outsmarted her. Sarah realized she still had the hydrogen

peroxide. She splashed it in Satan's head wound. He screamed. The slice seemed to bubble up and dissolve half of his face. When he tried to talk, his brain came out and the chemicals seemed to dismember his body and his vital organs ended up on the floor. Sarah cried out for her mother, to which there was no response. The house turned back to normal, and so did her life. But she'll never forget what's behind closed doors.

The Dead Body

The rope stood still. The man did not. He ran throughout the store, not managing to navigate through the dark building, and having no luck finding just the one thing he was looking for: help. The situation: 10:43 PM. The night guard saw a figure between isles F and G. Taking out his flashlight and pistol from his drawer, he felt something unfamiliar. Dread. As the handle of the door behind him clicked, and he felt cold air rush upon him, he spun around to see a strange person standing amidst him. The figure frightened the man. It had eyes wide open, and its lips were parted, as if to say, "oh." The figure held a rope in its left hand. The rope had an ankle-sized loop at the end. What do you expect? The figure threw the loop around the man's ankle and tightened it, and dragged him out of the room. Now, to answer your questions:

-Who is "The Man?" Answer: Dead
-Who is "The Figure?" Answer: Should have been dead.

How could the story possibly be told? Well, let's start it this way: Nicole. Age 17. A sweet, loving girl who did not deserve what she would soon get. Nicole would visit the town grocery store ever so often to fulfill the family's food and drink supply. The town grocery store was open 24/7, so Nicole would make late trips and return home just in time for supper. One night was an extra late trip, which wasn't the worst thing, but it also wasn't the best thing, because it was quite frightening there after dark. Nicole didn't believe in ghosts. Not until what happened. After tonight, the extra late trip, Nicole was reported missing. But really, she was in plain sight. How this happened? On that extra-late trip, tonight, Nicole got to the town grocery store, and noticed that the lights were off, which was very unusual. She decided they either wanted to save electricity or the power was out. The wooden sign showed that it was open, so Nicole reluctantly continued in. Opening the door, she caught an ever so slight whiff of a putrid odor, one that a dead animal would smell like. She suspected that a can of beans and pickles had spilled, since the two don't make a pleasant smell. The hairs on the back of her neck stood up straight. She expected someone to jump out at her at any second. Nicole had heard about and seen the mischievous 14-year-old who worked at the store. His name was Mike. Mike liked to scare people. He acted as a dead body and made people terrified. It almost got him fired on several occasions. His face mask made him a lot scarier. Mike's very recent death sparked up social media. He very mysteriously died in the store. But it was interesting: his body was never found. Just his head. It was severed, with its eyeballs hanging out, and the rest gruesomely bludgeoned inward. His brain wasn't found either. There hasn't been any more murders since then, but definitely some creepy things. Jeanie Bush saw a headless ghost wandering through the place, but Nicole thought that was made up. Bill Nostathe hosted a demonic ritual with his so-called "Fan Club" in hopes of satanizing

Mike's soul. Jerks. Then Nicole saw it. The figure. Between isles F and G. This time the figure didn't dash past; it stood still. It stood still and stared. Stared right through Nicole's soul. But she didn't scream. Instead, she grabbed the jar of pickles next to her. Unscrewed the cap. Poured out the food. She took a step toward it. Took another step. Another one. Once Nicole, very timidly, got close enough, she bashed the glass over the figure's head. It didn't show any sign of pain. Instead, it lunged at her. It pulled her hair. Nicole thrashed. Screamed. It pulled her into The Man's office and the door shut. Nicole heard a click. The door was locked. She banged and screamed at the door. There was no sound. There was a computer on the desk there that was constantly feeding a live stream of what was going on in the building. She used the light of the computer screen to see what the dark object under the desk was. Nicole leaned in close, and realized it was...a dead body. The dead body of The Man; the body of Josh Magnolin, the night security guard at the place, who went missing and was never found. In Josh's holster on his belt, there was no gun, but there was a crowbar. Nicole had not noticed before, but the wood on the door had been plied off; it seemed as if Josh's gun had been taken and replaced with a crowbar, which had been used to try and open the door. Then Nicole realized she had no escape; as month after month after month went by, she only survived by feeding on Josh's dead meat. When there was no more flesh to eat, she was left to mourn and die on that floor. But her soul lived on. Nicole's dead body arose and "browsed" the store. "The Figure" was future Nicole.

Him

What follows is a true story of
messing around with friends turned
into a hunt for the truth. When I
was in 4th or 5th grade, I had a
group of friends in which I would
always hang around. This group
consisted of 5-8 people. We were so
imaginative. I can remember all our
wild tales and and games, the
childhood memories that would last
forever. Yet--not every memory was
as bright as others. Some were
darker. Now, my friends and I
would always like a good scare. We

all were obsessed with ghosts, demons, monsters and would always try to hunt for these things in places we would normally go to. We knew, inside, that it was a joke. But it was not always that way. Let's take the day this story begins for example. School was dull as usual. I fought through math first (barely). When will we ever need to know what x represents? I mean, when in life will we ever have to solve $(xyz(29))$ x $(f57)$? I know, I know, we have to learn it. But why? Anyway, the next class was English. We basically read, which wasn't the worst, except for when I get called on to read. Ugh. Then after that class, there is... you guessed it... lunch and recess! Yay! Finally, we are free--if only for 30 minutes.

Then came social studies. World War 2, Germany gets revenge, Hitler blames America/Jews, the Holocaust... "Colin! What do you think about what Stella just said?" "Umm..." I sank down in my seat. "Yea, uh, the, uh, Holocaust was unfair... I--I mean, the submarine disasters while passing Germany! Um... Pearl Harbor?" My teacher looked at me like I was stupid. She was right. Ugh, I should have been paying attention! After class ended (there was no science that day because my social studies teacher also taught that, and she changed subjects weekly), one of my friends from the friend group handed out invitations to his birthday party. Obviously, I got one and read the invitation. It said that his party would take place at his uncle's house. I wondered why his uncle's house instead of his own, but didn't think much of it. The days following up to the party were not fully filled with excitement, mostly confusion and wondering about how long we would stay in the morning (it was a sleepover, too), and what the party would consist of. I believe the party was on a Saturday, but I'm not sure since it was so long ago. I will just say it was a Saturday. So, that Saturday, my parents drove me to my friend's uncle's house. I wasn't really expecting much, so when I got there, my family and I were awed. This house was nothing short of *magnificent*. It was a massive castle-like home with countless windows, doors, rooms, and cone-shaped pillars jutting out of the top of the place. It was a mansion. I entered through the big front door with my family, said my goodbyes and savored the sweet scent of the building. My friends greeted me by screaming, tumbling down the stairs, pushing my bags to the ground, grabbing my arm, and dragging me up the stairs. We went up a few stories, ran down a long, narrow hallway, turned a few corners then opened a small, wooden door which led to a little wooden spiral staircase. As I went up the spiral staircase with my friends, I realized this must be an attic, because it was very hot and humid. This attic was actually really cool. It had a couch, a television with at least a few consoles, a foosball table, a few nooks leading to windows, one of which had a great view of a pool. After showing me this man cave, my friends took my back down the spiral staircase and out that door to another hallway, into a little room with a few couches, then through a door in that room which led to the inside of one of the cone-shaped pillars. The inside of this pillar was a tall, circular library with a rolling ladder to reach the books at the top. This ladder was also used to get to the second story of this library, which was a place you could sit down to read. It had a bean bag for that. There were windows up there, too, and bright lights shining from these windows, like a watch tower. All the other rooms and stuff in this building were bedrooms bathrooms, and hangout rooms. I thought. Later that night, we had foosball competitions, pizza, drinks (sparkling grape juice-- right???). We mostly just joked around up in the attic, playing/ watching TV. We got a little rowdy, and when a few of our friends got too rough and were kind of being jerks, the rest of us ditched them and left them to horse around and be weird in the attic. The ones who were still sane (including me) went around exploring, because who knows what this house has to hide. We decided to split up, which was a good idea. After about 10 minutes of searching, we reported back to each other on how we had found nothing but how confusing this house was, like it was similar to the Winchester Mansion. We searched each floor, but still found nothing out of the ordinary. Near the time when we were giving up, one of my friends, let's call him Brad, said he had to go pee. After Brad left the bathroom, he reported to us excitedly that there was a strange door in the bathroom. We all went in there and another friend, let's call him Lucas, being the "head investigator," bravely opened the door to reveal a strange hallway. At the end of that hallway (and past a few turns), there was one door, which Lucas, again, opened, and behind it was an old bathroom. *Weird.* We asked the friend who invited us about it, let's call him Oliver, and he told us to ask his uncle. Oliver's uncle had never seen this either. This strange find restored our hope and our expeditions were renewed. We learned to pay closer attention to everything we saw. After maybe 5 minutes of detailed searching, Lucas, out of breath told us all to follow him. We followed him to a door that had been painted over and blended in to the wall in one of the bedrooms. Lucas found the handle, which was a metal ring, and pulled the heavy wooden door open. He urged me to go in and look instead of him, and I didn't want to embarrass myself, so I went in. It was very cold in there, probably about 30 degrees Fahrenheit. I instantly found myself surrounded by a ton of dolls and rocking chairs. As if that wasn't creepy enough, I heard the door slam behind me and my friends snickering. Then, as if on cue, one big, white rocking chair at the opposite end of the room, started to rock slowly. And there was something sitting in it. What looked like a Raggedy Anne doll. I had had enough. I pounded on the door and told my friends there was something in there with me. That was enough for them to understand that I was in danger, so they let me out. I explained the full story to them and we knew there was something sinister in that room. We hurried to the first story and told Oliver's uncle that there was a hidden room in the wall full of dolls and rocking chairs and that one of the chairs moved. He did not even believe that there was a room there until we brought him upstairs and into that room, then opened the door for him to be shocked. He didn't know his house as well as he thought he did. We decided we had done enough searching for the night, and that we should just relax and have fun. *We* decided that. Unfortunately for us, the *spirits* decided against it. Later, when the hyped-up crazy friends were after Lucas and I, we went into the pillar library. We hid behind the chairs and waited for them to go away. We were holding in laughter until I sensed the thing. I started sweating profusely, the air around me turning colder. I felt something stab me in the back while my throat got tighter. Something was choking me. I was able to hold my breath while Lucas attempted to fend of the demon. I thought it might kill me as the pain in my back grew worse and the air in my lungs was disappearing. Finally, it let go of me, but only when my other friends walked in the room. It didn't want to get caught. Lucas asked me if I was okay while I recovered from the pain. Lucas checked my back, and sure enough, there was a big scratch where I felt pain. We were shocked, and, for some reason, we went up to the second story and looked out the window. Just an urge, I guess. We saw a glimpse of a figure in the pool, but we couldn't be sure. So, we went up to the attic and into one of the nooks, and we were correct. There was a tall figure in the pool, staring right at us. We were all freaked out. I then had another weird urge to go and check the pillar library. As I reached the room to enter the library (alone), the rug leading into the library rolled out. It looked like the side view of ocean waves hitting the shore. I was scared and confused, and I felt like something *led* me through the bathroom, through the door, through the hallway, and into the secret bathroom. I noticed a little red stain in the bathroom floor as I curled up into a little ball next to the toilet and put my head down. I must have fallen asleep or something, because when I lifted my head up, I heard my Lucas and Brad calling my name. I yelled at them that I was in here, and they ran in with a worried look. "What are you doing in here?"

asked Lucas. "I--I'm not really sure." I replied. He helped me up and I told them about the rug and how I "had" to come here. I swore that I wouldn't wander off again, because something could get to me. Another thing: When Lucas helped me out of the bathroom, the word "HIM" was in my head. "HIM, HIM." I don't know, it was weird. Anyway, We spent the rest of the night having fun in the attic, and the sleeping arrangements were weird at first, and we all ended up sleeping in the same nook, which was crowded, while one of us slept on the couch. Let's call him Hudson. Hudson had a strange sleepwalking encounter in the middle of the night, but other than that, we just had fun, joked around, and didn't have another paranormal experience that night. In the morning, we ate breakfast, then got a ghost-hunting tool which tracked down ghosts and also served as a spirit box. The ghost radar found nothing in any of the floors above first floor. The spirit box did catch something though: it was something about rice. We rushed down to the freezer in the kitchen, where rice was kept, and a dot appeared on the radar. We followed the dot to the room to the right of the freezer (this room was in the kitchen), and we opened went into the room to find Oliver's uncle. We asked him if anything happened here, and he said, "Yes, in fact, I almost died here. A tree fell right in this exact spot, but thank God my wife and I were in our bedroom when it happened." This terrified us. The demon made this happen. *He* made this happen. My friends and I just hung around until my parents came to pick me up, and I told them everything, none of which they believed. I still cannot get them to believe me. But that is unimportant. What is important is what I'll never forget. And I'll never forget that word: *HIM.*

Made in the USA
Coppell, TX
08 January 2020

14262090R00022